Angel Falls

FACES
AND
PLACES

VENEZUELA

BY PATRICK MERRICK

THE CHILD'S WORLD®

COVER PHOTO

A Venezuelan boy in a straw hat.
©Pablo Corral V/CORBIS

Published in the United States of America by The Child's World®
PO Box 326
Chanhassen, MN 55317-0326
800-599-READ
www.childsworld.com

Project Manager James R. Rothaus/James R. Rothaus & Associates
Designer Robert E. Bonaker/R. E. Bonaker & Associates
Contributors Mary Berendes, Dawn M. Dionne, Katherine Stevenson, Ph.D., Red Line Editorial

The Child's World® and Faces and Places are the sole property
and registered trademarks of The Child's World®.

Library of Congress Cataloging-in-Publication Data
Merrick, Patrick.
Venezuela / by Patrick Merrick.
p. cm.
Includes index.
ISBN 1-56766-915-8 (lib. bdg. : alk. paper)
1. Venezuela—Juvenile literature. [1. Venezuela.] I. Title.
F2308.5 .M47 2002
987—dc21
00-013188

Table
of
Contents

CHAPTER	PAGE

Seen from high above, planet Earth has seven large land areas surrounded by oceans. These land areas are called **continents**. The nation of Venezuela lies at the northern end of the continent called South America.

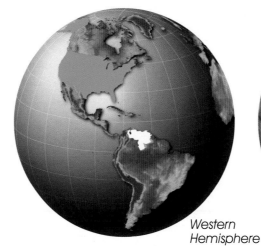

Western Hemisphere

Eastern Hemisphere

Venezuela (white) and U.S.A. (green) are both in the west

To the north Venezuela is bounded by the Caribbean Sea and the Atlantic Ocean. Neighboring countries are Guyana to the east, Brazil to the south, and Colombia to the west and southwest. Venezuela is just north of the **equator**, the imaginary line that divides Earth into two halves.

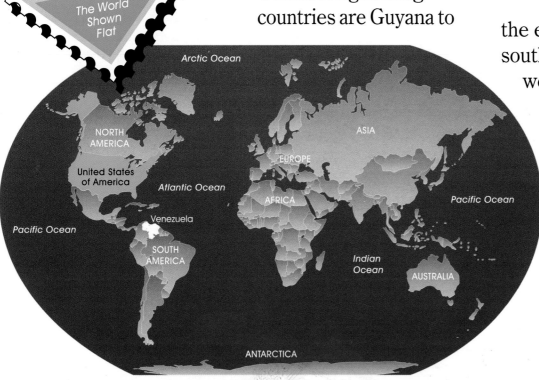

The World Shown Flat

Arctic Ocean

NORTH AMERICA

United States of America

Atlantic Ocean

Pacific Ocean

Venezuela

SOUTH AMERICA

ASIA

EUROPE

AFRICA

Indian Ocean

Pacific Ocean

AUSTRALIA

ANTARCTICA

Close-Up
Of
Venezuela

Caribbean Sea

Atlantic Ocean

VENEZUELA

GUYANA

COLOMBIA

BRAZIL

The
Coastline
At
Chichiriviche

Chichiriviche

ANDES

Angel Falls
CANAIMA
NATIONAL
PARK

©Pablo Corral V/CORBIS

A Waterfall In Canaima National Park

©Yann Arthus-Bertrand/CORBIS

Venezuela is a beautiful land. Along its seashore are scenic islands, sandy beaches, and stretches of steep coastline. The snow-capped peaks of the Andes Mountains cover the northwest part of the country.

A Small Mountain In Canaima National Park

©Yann Arthus-Bertrand/CORBIS

In the southeast are the Guiana Highlands, with their tall, flat-topped mountains. Hidden in these highlands is Angel Falls, the world's highest waterfall. Between the two mountainous regions lies a huge flat area of *llanos* (YAH-nos), or plains. This flat, treeless land is desertlike during the dry season but becomes green and swampy during the rainy season.

Venezuela's different types of land support a wide variety of plants and animals. The mountains have thick forests and beautiful flowers. The llanos are covered with seas of tall grass.

In all parts of Venezuela, bogs and marshes can be found near the lakes and rivers. The far southern portion of Venezuela lies near the equator, where the weather is always hot and sticky. Here the huge Amazon rain forest grows green and thick.

In each different area, wonderful and exotic animals make their homes. There are bears, jaguars, anteaters, and monkeys in the mountains. Brightly colored birds and snakes live in the forests. In fact, Venezuela is home to the world's longest snake, the anaconda. Off the coasts of Venezuela, shrimp, eels, and unusual fish swim through the warm waters and hide in the beautiful **coral**.

©Kevin Schafer/CORBIS

An Adult Jabiru (Center) With Young in The Llanos

©Pablo Corral V/CORBIS

LLANOS

MÉRIDA

Plants
Growing
In The
Mérida
Region

The Revolt Of Valencia In 1873

Valencia •

• San Antonio

©Bettmann/CORBIS

Long Ago

People have been living in Venezuela for thousands of years. The first people were Native Americans who lived by farming, hunting, and fishing. Some of these people built towns and complex societies.

©Christie's Images/CORBIS

Simón Bolívar

In 1498, Spanish explorer Christopher Columbus landed on Venezuela's beaches. Soon afterward, other Europeans came looking for gold and brought African slaves to work on farms. For the next 300 years, Spain ruled the entire area. In the early 1800s, famed leader Simón Bolívar led a fight that freed Venezuela and much of South America from Spanish rule.

An Old Spanish Fortress In San Antonio

©K. M. Westermann/CORBIS

Venezuela Today

Presidential Candidate Hugo Chavez Casting His Vote In Caracas

©AFP/CORBIS

In the early 1900s, huge oil deposits were found in Venezuela. A few Venezuelans made a great deal of money selling the oil to other countries. Most of Venezuela's people still lived in **poverty**, with barely enough money to live. After much fighting among themselves, the people of Venezuela finally took control of their own country. They established a **democracy** in which they could elect their own leaders.

Today, Venezuela is separated into states, just like the United States. Each state has a governor and can elect **representatives** and senators to make laws and help govern the country. Venezuelans elect a president, too. The nation also has a court system that tries to make sure all Venezuelans are treated fairly.

A Council Meeting In Chacao

©Pablo Corral V/CORBIS

Caracas ★ Chacao
Pedernales

An Oil Rig Near
Pedernales

©Yann Arthus-Bertrand/CORBIS

A Pemon
Man At
Angel Falls

Caracas   Mucutuy

Angel Falls

©Chris Rainier/CORBIS

The People

Because the native Indian people and the people from Europe have been living together for so long, most Venezuelans have mixed backgrounds. Some people are *mestizos* with both Indian and European relatives. Others are *pardos* with Indian, European, and African backgrounds.

A Man Selling Record Albums At A Caracas Market

©Pablo Corral V/CORBIS

For many Venezuelans, religion is very important. This can be seen in the education and the values of the country. Some people practice other religions, but most people are Roman Catholic. In fact, 9 out of every 10 Venezuelans belong to this faith.

A Family In Mucutuy

©Pablo Corral V/CORBIS

17

City Life And Country Life

ADMIT ONE

ADMIT ONE

Most Venezuelans live in or around larger cities. Venezuela's cities are much like cities in other countries. How people live in the city depends on the amount of money they have. Wealthier people live in nice apartments or houses. Many poor people live outside of town in a *rancho,* or slum, in houses made of old metal or cardboard.

The people remaining in Venezuela's countryside include Indian tribes who live in more hidden regions. There they live in simple houses and hunt and fish just as their ancestors did hundreds of years ago.

Today, much of the culture of these people is in danger. As the cities of Venezuela get larger, there is less room for the Native groups. The Native Indians are interacting more with the city dwellers. Many Indians now live on the outskirts of the cities in very poor living conditions.

People Rowing A Canoe In The Jungle

©Neil Rabinowitz/CORBIS

Caracas

An Aerial
View Of
Caracas

Young
Women Studying
In Caracas

La Guaira
Caracas

©Pablo Corral V/CORBIS

School in Venezuela is a lot like school in the United States. Students learn reading, writing, math, and science. After elementary school, students can go on to secondary school and then to study at one of the country's universities. All education, from kindergarten through college, is free.

Schools in the larger cities might look a lot like American schools, but schools in the countryside are very different. Some country-dwelling children cannot go to school because they must work with their parents instead. Others cannot go to school because there is no school where they live.

DESAYUNO CRIOLLO
PESCADO FRITO
HERVIDO DE PESCAD
EMPANADAS
REFRESCOS
JUGOS NATURALES

©Pablo Corral V/CORBIS

A Restaurant Menu Painted On A Wall In La Guaira

Students In A Library In Caracas

©Pablo Corral V/CORBIS

Spanish is the official language of Venezuela. In smaller villages, however, people still speak the Native Indian languages their relatives spoke hundreds of years ago.

A Man Working In A Print Shop In Mérida

©Pablo Corral V/CORBIS

Venezuelans work at many different types of jobs. In Venezuela's vast central plains, people work on farms. Because of the nice warm weather, they can grow many different kinds of food, such as sugarcane, bananas, and coffee. The same region has ranches where cowboys tend huge herds of cattle just as they did in the American Old West.

In the cities, many people work in factories that make clothes or other products. Others work in plants that pump and **refine** oil to sell to other countries. Other Venezuelans have jobs in banks, offices, shops, and restaurants.

Workers Selecting Coffee Beans In Santa Cruz De Mora

©Pablo Corral V/CORBIS

Mérida
Santa Cruz de Mora
LLANOS

Men Tagging
Calves In The
Llanos

A Woman
Grilling
Arepas
In Mérida

Caracas

Mérida

©Pablo Corral V/CORBIS

Food

Venezuelan foods reflect a wonderful mixture of Native American, European, and African cooking styles and flavors. One of the most important foods is the corn **arepa**, a flat, thick pancake often stuffed with a meat, cheese, or fruit filling.

Besides arepas, most meals include beans, tropical fruits, and coffee. Another favorite dish is *pabellon,* which is made with beef, black beans, rice, and bananas.

Besides traditional meals, Venezuelans also eat many different kinds of food. If you like seafood, you can find dishes made with fish or even shark! In the larger cities you can find more American foods, such as hamburgers or even pizza.

A Fruit Stand Near Caracas

Venezuelans love sports, including basketball, soccer, and especially baseball. Every town or village has a baseball field where children and adults play. Professional teams play each other and teams from other countries. Besides sports, many Venezuelans like to hike in the mountains or spend time at the beach. Shopping and simply spending time with friends and family are popular pastimes, too.

Holidays are very important in Venezuela. Most of these holidays celebrate religious events. The biggest holiday is Carnival, a two-day festival that takes place before the religious season of Lent. The entire country celebrates Carnival with fireworks, parades, games, and dances.

Perhaps someday you can visit Venezuela during Carnival or another colorful festival. If you do, you will find a country filled with wonderful sights and friendly people.

Men Playing Chess In Caracas

©Pablo Corral V/CORBIS

Maracaibo

Valencia

Caracas

Barquisimeto

San Francisco de Yare

Devil Dancers During The Feast Of Corpus Christi In San Francisco De Yare

Area
About 352,000 square miles
(912,000 square kilometers)—more than twice the size of California.

Population
About 23 million people.

Capital City
Caracas.

Other Important Cities
Maracaibo, Valencia, and Barquisimeto.

Money
The bolívar.

Official Name
The Bolivarian Republic of Venezuela.

National Song
"Gloria al bravo pueblo que el yugo lanzó," or "Glory to the Brave Nation That Shook Off the Yoke."

National Holiday
Independence Day on July 5th.

National Flag
Three stripes of yellow, blue, and red. The yellow stripe stands for the country's wealth, the blue represents the sea, and the red stands for the blood shed during the fight for independence. Seven white stars on the blue stripe represent the original provinces, or parts of the country.

Head of Government
The president of Venezuela.

A Tree Frog On A Plant

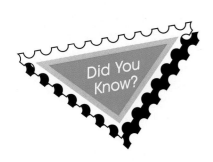

In the far northwest corner of Venezuela is Lake Maracaibo, South America's largest natural lake.

The Orinoco River flows through Venezuela's central llanos. It is home to many strange animals, including river dolphins, manatees, rare Orinoco crocodiles, and fish that weigh over 300 pounds.

Venezuela's population is growing. If you were to walk around in Venezuela, one out of every three people you'd meet would be a kid!

Although Venezuelans work hard, many still believe in taking a **siesta**, or midday rest. At noon, many stores close for two hours so people can go home for a big meal and a short nap. After the siesta, everyone goes back to work.

	SPANISH	HOW TO SAY IT
Hello	hola	OH–lah
Good-bye	adiós	ah–dee–OSE
Please	por favor	POR fah–VOR
Thank You	gracias	GRAH–see–uhs
One	uno	OO–noh
Two	dos	DOHS
Three	tres	TRACE
Venezuela	Venezuela	ben–ay–SWAY–lah

arepa (ah-RAY-pah)
An arepa is a flat, thick pancake-like bread made from corn. Arepas are often stuffed with meat, cheese or fruit.

continents (KON-tih-nents)
Earth's largest land areas are called continents. Venezuela is a country on the continent of South America.

coral (KOR-ull)
Coral are underwater structures made from the skeletons of tiny sea animals. Many coral formations lie in the ocean waters off the coast of Venezuela.

democracy (deh-MOK-reh-see)
A democracy is a type of government in which the people vote to choose their leaders. Both Venezuela and the United States have democratic governments.

equator (ee-KWAY-ter)
The equator is an imaginary line that runs around the middle of Earth and divides it into a north half and a south half. Countries on or near the equator have warm weather all year long.

poverty (POV-er-tee)
Poverty is the condition of being poor. Many Venezuelans live in poverty, with too little money for food, shelter, and other needs.

refine (ree-FINE)
When something is refined, unwanted things are removed from it. Some Venezuelans work at refining oil before it is sold to other countries.

representatives (rep-rih-ZEN-tuh-tivz)
Representatives are people chosen to speak or act for others. Venezuelans elect representatives who make laws for their country.

siesta (see-ESS-tah)
A siesta is a short rest or nap. Many Venezuelan people take a siesta after lunch.

Index

Web Sites

Learn more about Venezuela!

Visit our homepage for lots of links about Venezuela:
http://www.childsworld.com/links.html

Note to Parents, Teachers, and Librarians:
We routinely verify our Web links to make sure they're safe,
active sites—so encourage your readers to check them out!

DATE DUE

MAR 3 1 2009		
APR 2 8 2009		
OCT 2 3 2009		
NOV 0 3 2009		